Gary Grasshopper Meets Madison Mole

Written by Connie Amarel
Illustrated by Swapan Debnath

ISBN 978-1-61225-178-3

Published by Mirror Publishing
Milwaukee, WI 53214

Printed in the USA.

This book is dedicated to friends, new and old, who bless our lives in so many ways. It is lovingly dedicated to my beautiful grandnieces Amelia and Madison, my handsome grandnephew Glenn, and in memory of Auntie Florinda (“Tia Flea”) who is missed so much. It is also dedicated to my wonderful friends, Juanita Brown and Dr. Alan Weber, for their much appreciated suggestions, to my family for their love and support, and with deepest gratitude to my publisher, Neal, and illustrator, Swapan.

Gary Grasshopper looked up at the blue sky above and smiled happily. It was summer vacation and he was enjoying the bright, sunny day at the park.

Gary and his friends, Buster Beetle, Inchy Inchworm, and Tommy Termite, had come to the park to play kickball.

Gary was also excited because his best friend, Freddie Firefly, was coming to visit tomorrow and would be staying with him for the next two weeks.

Gary had lots of fun activities planned and was anxious to introduce Freddie to Florinda Flea and her best friend, Amelia Ant.

Gary met Florinda and Amelia at a school dance and thought they were so nice, as well as being great dancers. He knew Freddie would like them a lot, too.

There was going to be a summer dance at the school next weekend and Gary knew Freddie would want to go.

Gary stopped daydreaming just in time to see Inchy kicking the ball toward him. It was a great kick that sent the ball flying far out into the field.

Gary hopped as fast as he could, trying to get to the ball to catch it. He took a giant hop, but when he landed, he hopped right into a mole hole.

Down and down he went until he landed with a thump. It was very dark, as the only light was coming from the opening of the mole hole way above him.

He rubbed his eyes to try to see where he was at. He stood up and tried to hop, but he had sprained his ankle badly and was unable to stand.

Suddenly he heard a female voice asking him if he was okay. Gary could barely see her in the dim light, but told her his name and that he had fallen down the mole hole and hurt his ankle.

She told him her name was Madison Mole and that she was going to help him. She tried to help him stand, but she wasn't strong enough to support him. Madison decided she would have to go for help.

Just then her cousin, Gopher Glenn, came and asked what was going on. Madison explained that Gary must have fallen down the hole they had made when they were checking out the park last night.

Glenn said he would go for help and told Madison to stay with Gary until he got back. While they were waiting for help to arrive, Gary asked Madison if this was where she lived.

Madison explained that her family and the whole mole community had been forced to leave their homes in another field to look for a new place to live, and that was why she was here.

She told *Gary* that her last home was wonderful, but that the field she lived beneath was being excavated to have a shopping mall built with underground parking. All the mole families had to pack up and leave in a hurry.

Madison said they were hoping to find a new place to live that would be safe and where they wouldn't have to worry about equipment tearing up the ground.

She also told Gary that they had moved once before when she was very young. It had rained really hard for several days and the field they lived beneath had flooded and all the mole homes had flooded, too.

Gary felt so sorry for Madison, especially when she told him how hard it was to move and leave all the familiar surroundings.

She said it was hard having to sleep in a new bed and that she wished that they could find a home where they would never have to move again.

Gary had always thought it would be fun to live somewhere different, but now he realized how lucky he was to have lived in the same house all of his life.

He also thought about his best friend, Freddie Firefly, and how hard it had been for him to move away. Gary told Madison about Freddie and that he was coming to visit tomorrow.

He told her that at first Freddie was sad to leave all his friends when he moved far away, and that he had even had problems with a bully. But now the bully was his friend and he really liked where he lived.

Madison felt better after hearing about Freddie and knowing that there were others who had to move away and leave their homes.

Just then Madison's family arrived to help. She introduced her mom and dad to Gary. They gently helped him stand, supporting him so his leg wouldn't be injured any further.

They told Gary about an area not far away where they would be able to take Gary up to the park more easily.

Gary had been thinking about everything Madison had told him. Suddenly he had an idea. The land adjacent to the park where he and his friends played was a protected area.

Gary told Madison's parents that if they built their mole community under that protected land, they would never have to move again.

Madison Mole, her cousin Gopher Glenn, her mom and her dad all clapped their hands in delight to think that they would be able to have a home where they knew they would be safe.

They carefully supported Gary as they carried him up and out of the mole hole and back to the park.

Gary saw Buster, Inchy, and Tommy frantically searching for him. He called out to them and they ran over and hugged him. They had been so worried about him.

Gary told them about hopping into the mole hole and that he had sprained his ankle. He introduced them to his new friends that had so carefully helped him get back to the park.

They all hugged and then decided they would help Gary get back to his house where he could rest his ankle.

Gary's new friends and his old friends stayed and made dinner for him, all of them laughing and talking and getting to know each other.

Gary looked at them and smiled. He thought how lucky he was to have so many wonderful and caring friends.

But he knew his biggest smile would come tomorrow, when his best friend Freddie Firefly would be here, too!

CPSIA information can be obtained at www.ICGtesting.com
Printed in the USA
BVIW12n2232250115
384914BV00001B/4